ANTIOCH
- - SEP 2005

Magid Fasts
for Ramadan

I0702371

CONTRA COSTA COUNTY LIBRARY

by Mary Matthews
Illustrated by E. B. Lewis

CLARION BOOKS/New York

WITHDRAWN
3 1901 03793 1716

I wish to express my gratitude to Jamal Elias,
Professor of Religion at Amherst College,
for quickening and deepening my interest in Islam.
—M.M.

Clarion Books
a Houghton Mifflin Company imprint
215 Park Avenue South, New York, NY 10003
Text copyright © 1996 by Mary Matthews
Illustrations copyright © 1996 by E. B. Lewis

Illustrations executed in watercolor on Arches cold press 300-lb. watercolor paper
Text is 14/19-point Bembo

All rights reserved.

For information about permission to reproduce selections from this book,
write to Permissions, Houghton Mifflin Company,
215 Park Avenue South, New York, NY 10003.

Manufactured in China

Library of Congress Cataloging-in-Publication Data

Matthews, Mary, 1928–
Magid fasts for Ramadan / by Mary Matthews ; illustrated by E. B. Lewis.
p.   cm.
Summary: Magid, an eight-year-old Muslim boy in Cairo, is determined to celebrate Ramadan by fasting
despite the opposition of family members who feel that he is not yet old enough to fast.
ISBN 0-395-66589-2   PA ISBN 0-618-04035-8
[1. Ramadan—Fiction. 2. Fasts and feasts—Islam—Fiction. 3. Cairo (Egypt)—Fiction.]
I. Lewis, Earl B., ill. II. Title.
PZ7.M43423Mag   1996
[Fic]—dc20   95-10452
CIP
AC

SCP 10 9 8 7 6 5 4

For Gary
—*M.M.*

To Rashida, my dear friend,
who is blessed with wisdom and understanding
—*E.B.L.*

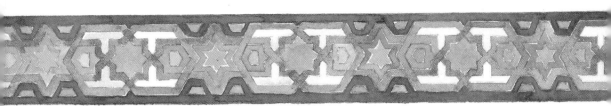

1.

Magid woke while it was still dark. He could hear the roosters crowing and the high, wavering voice of the muezzin calling people to prayer. "Allah is most great! Allah is most great! Come to prayer! Come to prayer!" chanted the muezzin from the top of the minaret. It would soon be morning.

The ceiling above Magid's head creaked. Giddu was getting his prayer rug. Magid pulled the sheet over his ears. But now he could hear his parents talking in the kitchen. Mama and Baba had gotten up to pray too. Or had little Ibrahim wakened them?

Then Magid remembered. Today was the first day of Ramadan, the month when good Muslims eat nothing and drink nothing all day, every day, from sunrise to sunset. Mama and Baba had gotten up to eat the last meal before daybreak. Magid wished he could fast too, but Mama and Baba said he wasn't old enough.

Magid sat up in bed. "I *am* old enough!" he thought. "I'm almost eight."

Last night, sitting with his grandfather on the verandah swing, watching the new moon, Magid had begged him, "Giddu, tell me the story of why we fast in Ramadan!"

"It was in the month of Ramadan," Giddu began, "on the Night of Power, that the Quran was first revealed to the Prophet Muhammad (may the peace and blessings of Allah be upon him!)."

"What happened, Giddu?" Magid nestled closer.

"The Prophet was praying in a lonely cave, high in the Arabian mountains, when the angel Gabriel appeared to him."

"And what did Gabriel say?" asked Magid, although he knew the story by heart.

"'Read! Read!' said the angel, but Muhammad didn't know how to read. He was frightened." Giddu pretended to tremble.

"Gabriel took hold of the Prophet and pressed him in his arms. He squeezed him three times, and again he said, 'Read!'" Giddu squeezed Magid three times, but not very hard.

"When the angel left," Giddu said, "the Prophet was shaking with fear."

Giddu pushed the swing to and fro with his foot. His eyes were looking far away.

"I can read," Magid said quietly. It was strange that the Prophet couldn't read, not even when he was a grown man, not even though he was the Messenger of God. Giddu was silent.

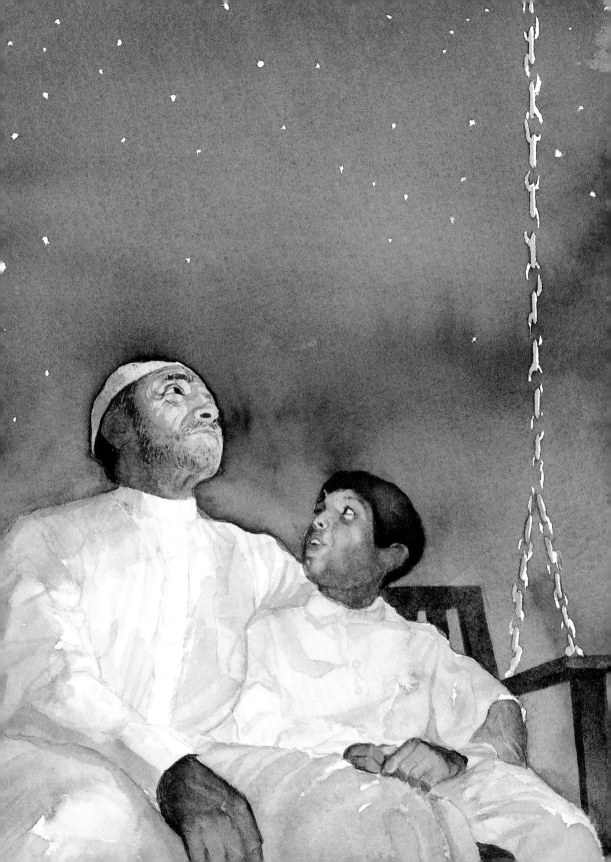

After a while Magid asked, "But why do we fast, Giddu?"

"The Quran tells us to fast," Giddu answered. "Fasting teaches us self-control, and it reminds us that everyone is equal before Allah, because we all feel hunger and need food."

"I want to fast this year," Magid said, "but Mama and Baba won't let me."

Giddu smiled. "You will fast when you are older," he said. "You will be a truly obedient Muslim and fast with all your heart. By then, Ramadan will fall in the winter, when the days are cooler and fasting is easier for all of us."

Last night, Magid had fallen asleep wondering at the strange way Ramadan slipped backward through the seasons. Now, sitting in bed, hugging his knees to his chest, he pictured his grandfather's face, all folds and furrows, like the sand in the desert.

"I want to be a truly obedient Muslim, like Giddu," Magid thought, and he whispered into the darkness, so that only Allah could hear him, "I am going to fast for Ramadan." Then he got out of bed.

As he pulled on his shorts, Magid heard his sister, Aisha, opening and closing drawers in her room. Surely Aisha wasn't getting dressed for school already! Now she was twelve she rode the bus to a girls' school in town, but she didn't leave this early.

Magid opened his bedroom door. There was a light on in the kitchen. He went in, rubbing his eyes.

"What are *you* doing out of bed?" Mama exclaimed. She was rinsing glasses in the sink.

"The muezzin woke me," Magid said. "Have you eaten the last meal already?"

Mama nodded, her forehead pinched into a frown. More banging and scraping were coming from Aisha's room.

"Why is Aisha up so early?" Magid asked.

"She got up for the *suhoor* meal. She's fasting this year," Mama said. "Had you forgotten?"

Magid's face fell. He *had* forgotten. And Aisha didn't even want to fast! But Baba had said she must, now she was going to the big Muslim school in the city. "I don't want my daughter to be the only Muslim in the school not fasting," Baba had said.

Magid didn't want to be the only member of his family not fasting. He went to his mother and wrapped his arms around her. "Mama!" he pleaded. "Can't I miss breakfast, even?"

Mama hesitated, clicking her tongue. "Oh, I suppose so!" she said at last. "For today. But you must go back to bed for at least two more hours!"

"I will, Mama," Magid said.

Aisha came into the kitchen, carrying her school satchel. Loose ends of hair stuck out of her braid all the way down her back. She glowered at Magid.

"What are you doing up?" she asked.

"Fasting," Magid said.

"You can't. You're too little."

"Mama said I could miss breakfast," Magid said.

"Pooh!" Aisha said. "That's nothing!" She sat down at the table and rested her head on her satchel.

Mama put her arm around Aisha's shoulders. "Aisha, dear," she said, "school doesn't start any earlier just because it's Ramadan. Go and rest on your bed a little longer!"

Aisha left, trailing her satchel. Magid was leaving too when Baba came in.

"*Sabahal-khair!*" Baba greeted them all cheerfully. He propped his medical journal against the empty coffee pot and sat down to read it.

"*Sabahan-noor!*" Magid called from the hallway, smiling to himself. Even Baba must be a bit rattled this first morning of Ramadan. He had buttoned his shirt buttons into the wrong buttonholes.

When Magid got up for the second time that day, Aisha had left for school. Baba had gone to the clinic. Only Mama and baby Ibrahim were home. It seemed strange to go to school without having breakfast first.

2.

As he was walking to school, Magid met a friend from his class, Gamal. Gamal was eating dried dates.

"Aren't you fasting for Ramadan?" Magid asked him.

"Of course not!" Gamal said. "Kids don't have to."

"I haven't eaten anything since last night," Magid said proudly. "My sister is fasting too."

Gamal shrugged his shoulders. "Our family doesn't fast much," he said and ate another date.

Magid was shocked. Then he remembered that Gamal's family didn't always go to Friday prayers at the mosque. Perhaps they weren't truly obedient? But *he* was going to be truly obedient, like Giddu.

All morning, instead of paying attention to his lessons, Magid thought about how to skip lunch. It was no use asking Mama for permission to miss lunch as well as breakfast, because she would say, "Little boys need to eat and grow strong." No, he had to find another way to fast.

By the time Magid returned home in the middle of the day, it was very hot. Normally, he would have gone straight to the kitchen for a glass of water, but you weren't supposed to drink if you were fasting. He went to find Mama. She had just finished feeding Ibrahim and was trying to get him to go to sleep. There were beads of sweat on her face.

"Let me look after Ibrahim, Mama!" Magid said. He picked up his little brother, who was almost too heavy for him to carry. "I'll take him into the yard and show him the hens." If he stayed outside for a while, perhaps Mama would forget to give him lunch.

The hens were sitting in the dust under the olive tree. Magid stood in the shade too, jiggling Ibrahim up and down. Then he caught sight of some geese in the irrigation ditch, floating on the muddy yellow water where the gray olive leaves brushed its surface.

"Look, Ibrahim!" Magid said. "Geese!"

Ibrahim laughed and stretched out his fat little hands toward the big orange-billed birds.

Magid's arms were starting to ache. He couldn't hold his brother much longer. He carried Ibrahim indoors again. But seeing the geese had given him an idea.

Mama had already put his lunch out on the kitchen table— bread and *halawa,* and a glass of lemonade.

"Is it all right if I take my lunch outdoors?" Magid asked.

"Of course!" Mama said. "Just be quiet when you come back in. Try not to wake the baby."

Magid carried the plate and glass to the bottom of the yard. As he went, he kept looking over his shoulder. He knew Mama was putting Ibrahim to sleep in the bedroom, but he felt as if her eyes were following him.

At the bottom of the yard, Magid sat down on the old bench under the olive tree. He held his lunch on his lap and looked at it. He was very thirsty, thirstier than he remembered ever being, and hungry too. He didn't really *have* to fast for Ramadan. In fact, everyone expected him not to.

Then Magid remembered what he had whispered to Allah in the early-morning darkness. He had promised Allah he would fast.

Magid looked around one last time. He was alone. There was no one to see. Quickly he tore up his sandwich, carried the plate over to the irrigation ditch, and swept the pieces off into the muddy water. The geese gobbled them up in an instant.

It was harder not to drink any of the lemonade, but Magid closed his eyes tight and poured it all out onto the ground. Then he walked slowly back to the house.

Magid left the plate and glass on the verandah and went to his room. He didn't want to talk to Mama just now. He was proud to be fasting for Ramadan, but in his heart he knew that she and Baba would be very upset if they found out.

3.

By the end of the afternoon, Magid's throat was parched and his skin, from the back of his neck to the soles of his feet, felt burning hot. When he heard the tap running in the bathroom he wanted to rush in, fill the largest glass he could find, and drink it all up at once. But he remembered his promise to Allah. He ran his tongue over his dry lips.

He didn't want to play with his cars any longer. Bending over them on the floor made him feel dizzy. He sat on the edge of his bed and rested his head in his hands. He felt weak, as if he had a fever. Did he have a fever? Then he wondered if Aisha felt the same way.

When Aisha came home and Magid heard her go into her room, letting the door bang, he crept down the hall and knocked timidly.

"Go away!" Aisha shouted.

Magid hesitated. Then he opened the door a crack. "Can I come in for a minute?" he asked.

Aisha didn't answer. Magid went in. Aisha lay stretched out on her bed. Her satchel and sandals lay where she'd dropped them.

"Have you had a hard day?" Magid asked.

"Terrible," Aisha said, with a groan. "Do you know, some of the girls weren't even fasting? We had to watch them eat lunch. It was horrible!"

"How do you feel now?" Magid asked. "Do you have a headache?"

"Yes, I do," Aisha said, pulling the pillow over her face. "A splitting headache. Please go away, Magid. You're lucky you're not fasting."

Magid grimaced. He tiptoed out of the room and closed the door quietly behind him. Baba, home already from the clinic, passed him in the hallway.

"I'm going to lie down for a while," Baba said, mopping his neck with a handkerchief. "Try to be quiet." He went into the bedroom, leaving the door open to catch the air from the hall fan.

Magid could hear Mama in the kitchen. He could smell onions cooking. His belly rumbled, but he didn't dare go into the kitchen. He couldn't bear to see the food, and he didn't want Mama asking awkward questions. He'd better do the same as Baba. Leaving his own door ajar, he lay down on his bed.

The hall fan clicked and whirred. Slowly the daylight faded.

Magid must have dozed. He was wakened by the creaking of the stairs that led to Giddu's apartment. He jumped up and ran to open the door. Giddu came in, wearing a clean white robe and a little crocheted cap.

"Giddu!" Magid cried. "Are the Ramadan lanterns lit?" From Giddu's apartment it was possible to see the top of the minaret. To let people know when the day's fast was ended, the muezzin would light lanterns there, although Baba preferred to listen for the announcement on the radio.

"Do you want to come up and watch for the Ramadan lanterns with me?" Giddu asked.

Magid slid his hand into Giddu's, and together they climbed the steep stairs to Giddu's apartment. Without putting on the light, Giddu sat down in a chair by the window, and Magid clambered onto his lap. It was getting quite dark. The sun had left a dusty purple haze in the sky. Then Magid saw a small light flicker and wink up near the top of the minaret. "Look, Giddu! Look!" he whispered. The muezzin was beginning to light his lamps.

"Let's go down and tell the others!" Magid said, tugging Giddu to his feet.

As they washed their hands, faces, and feet in the bathroom in preparation for the prayers, Magid heard the muezzin's high, wavering cry, just as he had heard it before daybreak. "God is most great! God is most great! Come to prayer! Come to prayer!"

Soon Baba and Aisha came into the living room, and then Mama, untying her apron.

Standing on the prayer rug next to Giddu's, Magid tried to follow everything his grandfather did and said. He knew most of the verses from the Quran he was supposed to recite, but he sometimes forgot when to stand and when to kneel, which shoulder to look over first, and how long to keep his forehead on the rug.

After they had finished the prayers, Baba rubbed his hands together. "Now let's eat!" he called in a hearty voice.

"The dates first!" Mama said, and they each took a date from the bowl Mama held out to them, breaking their fast the way the Prophet had broken his. Then Aisha brought glasses of cold water from the kitchen. Magid drank his all at once. It was strange to eat and drink again.

Mama always prepared especially good dishes for the *iftar* meal during Ramadan. Tonight she had made lamb stew and milk pudding sweetened with honey. Magid held out his plate. He was blissfully content.

"Look what came in the mail today," Baba said after they had been eating for a while. He drew a thin blue air letter from his pocket.

"Is it from Uncle Samir in Detroit?" Aisha asked.

Baba nodded. "Samir wants to wish us a blessed Ramadan. They are fasting too."

"Even Haider?" Magid asked. Cousin Haider was only a year older than he was.

"No, not Haider. He's too young. Besides, it's very difficult to fast when you live in a non-Muslim country, though Samir says there are more Muslim children in Haider's school now than there used to be."

"My friend Esmad lived in America when she was little," Aisha said. "She had to go to school on Fridays."

"They have Saturday and Sunday off," Mama said, "so they can go to church or synagogue. You have Friday off so you can go to community prayers at the mosque."

Magid had stopped eating. Friday. The day after tomorrow. He and Aisha would both be home from school. How could he keep his secret from her? Then he saw Aisha staring at him. He quickly took a third helping of lamb stew.

"Why are you so hungry, Magid?" Aisha said in a loud voice. "Anyone would think you'd been fasting too."

Magid held his breath, but Baba was calmly folding up the air letter and Mama had gone to get the milk pudding. Magid looked across the table at Giddu. Giddu smiled serenely.

All the same, Magid felt uneasy. Could Aisha possibly *know*?

4.

On the second day of Ramadan, Mama allowed Magid to miss breakfast again, although she refused to wake him for the *suhoor* meal.

"You must get a proper night's sleep," she said.

Magid managed to wake anyway on Thursday. But on Friday he slept right through *suhoor.* When he went into the kitchen, he found Mama and Aisha cleaning Ramadan lanterns and putting new candles inside them.

"Can we go and sing for the neighbors tonight?" Magid asked, forgetting for a moment how much he wanted a glass of juice.

"For a little while," Mama said. "Do you remember the Ramadan song?"

"I remember the chorus," Magid said. "*Wahawi ya wahawi.* But I don't remember the rest." Mama laughed. Aisha began to hum the tune.

"Do you think Mrs. Diab will give us nuts again?" Magid asked.

"Maybe," Mama said.

"But you can't eat them until after *iftar*," Aisha said.

"I know," Magid said. "I'm not stupid." He picked up a cloth and began to polish. Soon the little lanterns, made of bright tin and colored glass, shone and glowed.

"The lanterns are the best part of Ramadan," Magid said.

"What I like best is getting new clothes at the end," Aisha said. "Are we going to Aunt Zaynab's for Eid al-Fitr this year, Mama?"

"Only if you behave like good children all the way through Ramadan." Mama waved her finger at them. Magid was pleased. He liked to go to Cairo to see Aunt Zaynab and Uncle Rasheed and his cousins, Omar and Magda. If they were lucky, Uncle Rasheed would take them to one of the street fairs. And for the feast they would eat roast chicken and stuffed grape leaves, baklava and sugar cakes. He would drink glass after glass of tamarind.

The thought of all the good things Eid al-Fitr would bring made Magid's empty belly ache. What a long time it was till the end of Ramadan! What a lot of fasting he still had to do! He was beginning to feel weak again already. Then Magid remembered the stories Giddu had told him about the Prophet—how, when he was still a little boy, Muhammad had worked as a shepherd in the Arabian wilderness, where it wasn't always possible to find food and water when you needed them. Even the Prophet knew what it was like to be weak with hunger and thirst. Hunger made everyone equal, that's what Giddu had said.

"The Prophet understands," Magid thought. "And so will Giddu when I tell him at the end of Ramadan. He will be proud of me then." The thought made Magid feel stronger. But today was going to be especially difficult, because Aisha was home, and he would have to make sure she didn't find out what he did with his lunch.

After noonday prayers, Baba went to visit an old patient who lived nearby, and Mama told Aisha to do her homework. Then she made Magid's lunch. Magid took it outside, but as he passed the verandah, Aisha came out, carrying her satchel. Magid's heart sank. From the verandah, Aisha could see all the way to the bottom of the yard.

"If I were you," Magid called to her, "I wouldn't try to read out here in the sun. You'll get a headache."

To his relief, Aisha went indoors. Magid hurried to the bottom of the yard. Then he heard the verandah door open again. He hid behind the olive tree and peeked out. Aisha had brought a sunshade out with her. She was sitting on the verandah swing with the sunshade open over her head. Her face was in shadow. He couldn't tell whether she was looking at him or not.

Magid pressed his back against the tree. The geese paddled about in the yellow-brown water at his feet. He held his breath. All was quiet save for the snorting of the geese as they waited to be fed.

Magid looked over his shoulder. Surely the olive branches hid him from the house? Quickly he tore up his sandwich and scraped the pieces into the water.

"What are you doing?" Aisha's voice shrilled in Magid's ear. He dropped the plate. It floated down through the water and settled into the yellow mud at the bottom.

"Now look what you made me do!" Magid wailed. "Sneaking up on me like that!"

"*I* made you? What were *you* doing? That's what Mama will want to know. You haven't been giving your food to the geese every day, have you? Is that why you've been so hungry at *iftar*? What are you up to, Magid?"

"I'm fasting," Magid said, choking back a sob.

"That's ridiculous!" Aisha said. "A little kid like you! And you've lost one of Mama's plates. I'm going to tell!" Aisha flounced back into the house, clattering the shutters behind her. Magid poured out the lemonade and carried the empty glass indoors. Mama met him in the kitchen. Aisha, standing behind her, gave him a smug look as he came in.

"What's this Aisha tells me?" Mama's voice was stern. A deep frown lined her forehead. "Giving your lunch to the geese? You've been going all day without food?"

Magid hung his head. "I'm fasting," he whispered.

"Oh, Magid, that isn't the way to fast! That's very disobedient. I should never have said you could miss breakfast. We need to talk about this when Baba gets home. And I want Giddu to be there too. Go to your room now. You too, Aisha. Even if your brother misbehaves, that's no excuse to be unkind to him. I'm disappointed in both of you." Mama pursed her lips and shook her head.

Slowly Magid followed Aisha out of the kitchen. Her shoulders were drooping and she didn't look at him as they went down the hall.

5.

As Magid waited with a heavy heart for Baba to come home, he thought about Ramadan, and about Giddu. He'd always pictured Giddu's look of pride when he found out that Magid had fasted like everyone else. But when Giddu learned that Magid had deceived Mama and Baba, Giddu wouldn't be proud of him at all. Why hadn't he thought of that?

It wasn't even clear he could go on fasting for a whole month anyway. It was too much for him. He should have been satisfied with missing breakfast. Magid gave a deep sigh. It was more difficult than he'd imagined to be a truly obedient Muslim.

There was a knock at his bedroom door. Then the door opened part way and Aisha stuck her head inside.

"You're to come to the living room," she said. "Baba and Giddu are there. Mama told them."

Aisha looked over her shoulder. Then she stepped inside Magid's room and closed the door behind her.

"Listen, Magid," she said. "I'm sorry I told on you. I think it's impressive, really, the way you went without food like that when you didn't have to. But they were bound to find out sooner or later."

Magid shrugged. He didn't feel like talking to Aisha right now.

"I'm in trouble too, you know," Aisha said, opening the door again.

Dejectedly, Magid followed her down the hall to the living room. Mama, Baba, and Giddu were waiting there.

"Magid," Baba said, "you've behaved very deceitfully. That isn't the way to celebrate Ramadan, is it?"

Magid hung his head. "No, Baba!" he said in a small voice. "But I wanted so much to fast." His lips started to tremble. "I told Allah I would. And everyone else was fasting—even Aisha." Silently Magid began to cry.

Then Giddu stood up and drew Magid close to his side. "Allah is generous," Giddu said. "Magid will be a truly obedient Muslim."

Magid rubbed his sleeve across his eyes and stared up at his grandfather. How could Giddu say that now?

"Truly," Giddu said. "You have fasted with all your heart, Magid, and you didn't give up when you discovered how hard it is. But it is important for a Muslim to be honest, and you weren't being honest, were you?"

Magid looked down again and shook his head. There was nothing he could say.

After a long silence, Giddu said, "Do you still want to fast, Magid?"

Magid's heart skipped a beat and he heard Mama gasp. Did he want to fast? What would happen if he said yes?

Then Magid thought of getting up tomorrow, and the next day, and the day after that, and going to school, and not eating, day after day until the end of Ramadan. No. It was impossible. Mama and Baba were right. He was still too young.

"No," Magid said at last. "Fasting all day is too hard." He raised his eyes to meet Giddu's. "But I think I could go without breakfast."

Magid looked at Mama. She was smiling, as if she were pleased with him, even proud.

"What does Baba say?" Giddu asked.

Before Baba could speak, Aisha cried out, "Oh, Baba, fasting all day is too hard for me too! Can't *I* fast part of the day this year, until I get used to it? Can't I break my fast when I get home from school?"

"I think she's right, dear," Mama said. "We've been too hard on her, insisting she fast like an adult when she's only twelve."

Baba stroked his chin thoughtfully. "Very well, then," he said. "Magid will fast until noon, and Aisha will break her fast before *iftar*. That is the best arrangement, I believe."

Mama nodded.

"What do you think, Giddu?" Magid asked anxiously.

Still holding Magid close to his side, Giddu reached out his other arm and drew Aisha close to him also.

"I'm very proud of you all," he said.

Then Mama told Magid and Aisha they must kiss each other and be friends. Magid drew back.

"Come on, Magid!" Aisha said, holding out her arms. "If it weren't for you, I'd still be fasting all day."

Magid grinned. "So would I," he said, "if it weren't for you!" He held up his face, and he and Aisha kissed each other on both cheeks, the way grownups do.

A Note on Islam

There are more than 900 million Muslims in the world. About 150 to 200 million live in Arab countries, and there are large Muslim populations in Pakistan, the Balkans, Indonesia, and parts of Africa, including Egypt, where this story is set. There are 3 to 4 million Muslims in the United States, of whom roughly 30 percent are African-American.

The Muslim faith is called Islam, and Muslims use the Arabic word for God, Allah. Abraham, Moses, and Jesus are all considered prophets by Muslims, and there are stories about them in the Quran, Islam's sacred text, but the final, most important prophet is the Prophet Muhammad.

Muhammad was born in Mecca, in what is now Saudi Arabia, in the year A.D. 571. He was raised by desert nomads. When he grew up he became a trader and was known as *al-Amin*, "the honest one." After he received a number of special revelations from God, Muhammad went to Medina with his Companions and founded Islam there in A.D. 622. Within a hundred years, Islam had spread eastward through Arabia and Persia to India, and westward through North Africa to Spain and parts of France and Italy.

Besides fasting during Ramadan, Muslims are expected to pray five times a day, to give money to support the poor, to make at least one pilgrimage to Mecca, and to make a profession of faith ("There is no God but God and Muhammad is the Messenger of God"). Muslims must not eat pork or drink alcohol.

On Fridays, Muslims gather for communal prayer in the mosque, their place of worship. There are no images of God in the mosque, but it may be beautifully decorated with colored tiles and elaborate calligraphy.

Worshippers take off their shoes before entering. In the mosque, prayers are led by an Imam, someone who is regarded by the community as especially wise and pious. There are no priests in Islam. Muslims always face toward Mecca when they pray.

The Islamic calendar is a lunar calendar. A lunar year has only 354 days and is not based on the earth's rotation round the sun, so it is unrelated to the progression of the seasons. That is why the ninth month of the Islamic calendar, Ramadan, may fall in the summer one year and in the winter some years later. On the Western calendar, it begins eleven days earlier each year.

In Egypt during Ramadan, children light small lanterns and sing Ramadan songs at home, and sometimes in the streets. People may give them nuts, deliciously roasted and seasoned, or special candies. Traditionally, children get new clothes at Ramadan. Favorite foods are prepared for the *iftar* and *suhoor* meals, eaten during the hours of darkness. Ramadan ends with Eid al-Fitr, a joyous feast, when family members visit one another and exchange gifts.

Glossary and Pronunciation Guide

Because some sounds in Arabic have no equivalent in English, these pronunciations are approximate. In Egyptian Arabic, the g in *Gamal, Giddu,* and *Magid* is like the g in *give.*

Aisha (EYE-sha): a girl's name
Allah (al-LAH): the Arabic word for God
Baba (BAH-ba): Daddy, Dad
baklava (BAK-la-VA): a dessert made from thin layers of pastry, nuts, and
    honey (in Arabic pronounced bak-LAH-wa)
Eid al-Fitr (EED-al-FITr): the festival at the end of Ramadan (literally, "the
    festival of the breaking of the fast")
Gamal (ga-MAHL): a boy's name
Giddu (GID-doo): Grandpa

halawa (ha-LAH-wa): a sweet spread made of crushed sesame seeds and honey

Ibrahim (IB-rah-HEEM): a boy's name, the Arabic form of Abraham

iftar (iff-TAHR): the first meal after sunset during Ramadan

Islam (iss-LAM): the Muslim religion (literally, "submission to the will of God")

Magid (MAH-gid): a boy's name

Mama (MAH-ma): Mommy, Mom

minaret (MIN-a-RET): a tall slender tower from which the call to prayer is made

mosque (MOSK): the Muslim place of worship (in Arabic, *masjid*—MASS-jid)

muezzin (moo-EZZ-in): the person who calls Muslims to prayer five times a day (in Arabic pronounced moo-ETH-in)

Quran (kur-AHN): the sacred book of Islam

Ramadan (ra-ma-DAHN): the ninth month of the Islamic calendar, during which Muslims fast between sunrise and sunset each day

sabahal-khair (sa-BAH-hal-HAIR): Good morning!

sabahan-noor (sa-BAH-han-NOOR): The response to sabahal-khair: Good morning!

suhoor (suh-HOOR): the last meal before sunrise during Ramadan

tamarind (TAM-a-rinnd): a tart drink, like lemonade, made from the tamarind fruit

wahawi ya wahawi (wa-HAH-wi ya wa-HAH-wi): nonsense words used as a refrain, like "tra-la-la"